VAMPIRE
STATE BUILDING

VAMPIRE STATE BUILDING

ELIZABETH LEVY

ILLUSTRATED BY
SALLY WERN COMPORT

HarperCollins*Publishers*

www.harperchildrens.com

Library of Congress Cataloging-in-Publication Data
Levy, Elizabeth.
     Vampire State Building / Elizabeth Levy ; illustrated by
Sally Wern Comport.
          p.   cm.
     Summary: Eleven-year-old Sam Bamford's on-line chess
pal is in New York to play in a tournament, but Sam's brother
and cousin are wary because Vlad has pointy teeth, comes
from Romania, and admits to keeping secrets.
     ISBN 0-06-000054-6 — ISBN 0-06-000053-8 (lib. bdg.)
     [1. Chess—Fiction.   2. Contests—Fiction.   3. Vampires—
Fiction. 4. Empire State Building (New York, N.Y.)—Fiction.
5. New York (N.Y.)—Fiction.]   I. Comport, Sally Wern, ill.
II. Title.
PZ7.L5827 Vam 2002   2002018934
[Fic]—dc21

Typography by Andrea Vandergrift
1 2 3 4 5 6 7 8 9 10
❖
First Edition

Dedicated to New York City

CONTENTS

AUTHOR'S NOTE

I live downtown in New York City, and from one window in my apartment I have a wonderful view of the Empire State Building. It's my favorite building in New York. Here's to Josh Danziger and Matthew Hardin, who, when we visited the Observation Deck on the eighty-sixth floor, took pictures of a pigeon pooping and gave me an idea for a scene in this book.

From another window in my apartment, I used to see the World Trade Center buildings. From my terrace, I watched that terrible day when they disappeared.

By September 11, 2001, I had handed in this book to HarperCollins, and my wonderful and thoughtful editor, Ruth Katcher, had just finished what we thought were the final notes. While I was doing the rewrite, I tried to imagine and add what Sam and Robert would have felt about showing off their hometown, New York, a year after the tragedy, when I knew this book would be coming out.

I grew up in Buffalo, New York, but New York City has been my home for almost forty years. I've explored almost every inch of it by bicycle, on foot, and by subway, and I love taking my nieces, nephews, godchildren, and the children of my friends on my explorations with me. New York has always been a place where strangers talk to each other and share a moment or a joke. But after September 11, we all shared more. We all asked each other, "Are you all right? Is your family okay?" I'm writing this a month after the tragedy in the hope that my readers will share some of Sam's and Robert's love of New York—as well as mine.

Elizabeth Levy
October 5, 2001

VAMPIRE
STATE BUILDING

1

CHESS NUTS

Eleven-year old Sam Bamford chewed his lower lip and stared at the chessboard glowing on his computer. Then he glanced out the window of his fourth-floor apartment. He could just see the lights on the top of the Empire State Building, brightening the skyline of New York City.

In downtown Bucharest, Romania, twelve-year-old Vlad Clinciu sat in his fourth-floor apartment, looking out at the ruins of a palace that was more than five hundred years old. Vlad wore a satisfied grin. "Your move!" he typed into his computer.

"I know . . . I know," Sam typed impatiently.

Vlad and Sam lived half a world apart. They had never met face-to-face. Chess had brought them together. Vlad and Sam had met through their schools in a special program for kids that let them play on-line chess with instant messages. Now, they played together all the time at home. Vlad had told Sam that he was a beginner, but for a beginner he was really, really good. Once again, Vlad had won.

"Checkmate," typed Vlad.

"You slayed me," Sam typed into his computer.

"I know. Sorry."

"No you're not," typed Sam.

"You're right, friend," Vlad replied. "I don't think Buddy Ryan is ever sorry when he beats somebody."

"Well, he's one American who can beat you," typed Sam. Buddy Ryan was a new chess whiz kid. The sixteen-year-old boy from Davenport, Iowa, was said to be the best American player in years. Both Vlad and Sam followed his matches on the Web.

2

"How about another game?" asked Sam.

"Yes, if my annoying sister, Nadia, doesn't bother me," wrote Vlad.

"She can't be more annoying than my brother, Robert, and cousin Mabel," typed Sam. "Right now, Mabel's over at my house. She and Robert are playing chess, but they're not any good."

"Let's hope they all leave us alone," wrote Vlad. He set up the on-screen board for a new game. Soon the boys were deep into it.

Vlad loved playing with Sam. They seemed to have so much in common, including having annoying siblings the same age. Vlad liked having an American friend to practice English with. Vlad and his family had lived in London, England, for two years when his father was on a trade mission there. Both Vlad and Nadia had quickly learned to speak English.

In New York, Sam studied the chessboard, determined to win this game. But before he could make his move, Robert and Mabel

3

came over to the computer desk, carefully carrying a chessboard and pieces. Mabel was dressed in red jeans, a red T-shirt, and red glitter sneakers. After she moved to New York from San Francisco, she decided she needed a signature style to show off her taste. Hers was that everything matched.

"Sam, I need help," begged Robert. "Mabel is going to beat me. I hate when she does that."

"I'm just the better player," said Mabel. "Face it."

"Go finish your game somewhere else," said Sam impatiently. "I've got to figure out a strategy to beat Vlad."

"You're always playing with Vlad," complained Robert. "You taught me this stupid game, and now you never play with me."

"Vlad from Romania." Mabel sighed. "It's so romantic."

"It's not romantic. He's just a cool chess player," said Sam.

"Did you know," said Mabel, "that the real Dracula came from Romania?"

"Vlad and I don't talk about Dracula,"

4

said Sam. "We talk about chess."

"Are you on-line now?" asked Mabel. "I want to ask Vlad a question about Romanian vampires."

"He's very busy," said Sam.

"What's going on?" typed in Vlad, noticing Sam's silence.

"My annoying cousin and my little brother are interrupting," Sam typed in. "They are pests."

"Pests?" asked Vlad. "What's a pest?"

"Let me talk to him!" whined Mabel.

"They're insects masquerading as people," Sam wrote back. "Here, one of them wants to say hello."

"My little sister is a pest, too," wrote Vlad.

"We will have to get pest control," wrote Sam, and added the letters LOL for "laughing out loud."

Mabel was reading over Sam's shoulder. She pushed Sam away from the keyboard. "Your sister won't like being called a pest. I bet she's nice," Mabel typed quickly. "What's her name? I'm Mabel. Can I e-mail her?"

"Her name is Nadia," wrote Vlad. "She's named after Nadia Comaneci, the great Romanian gymnast."

"Can she speak English? Maybe we can be friends."

"Yes, she lived in London, too," Vlad wrote back. "She is only nine years old. But I think she would like an e-mail friend in America." He added Nadia's e-mail address.

"I'm nine years old, too," wrote Mabel. "So is Sam's brother, Robert. And we are not pests."

"Give me back the keyboard," said Sam. "This is my private time on the computer. Will you two go away and play somewhere else?"

"Hey," said Robert. "Ask Vlad if he knows why you two should stay away from squirrels."

Sam sighed and typed the question to Vlad.

"Is this a joke?" Vlad asked.

"Yes, from my little brother," typed in Sam.

"Give me the keyboard," said Robert. Robert typed, "Because they like chestnuts, and you're a chess nut. Get it?"

"I've heard that joke before," typed in Vlad.

"All chess players know that chess joke," said Sam, looking over Robert's shoulder. "Now, you and Mabel get out of here. I've got to figure out how to get out of the trap that Vlad set."

"Come on, Robert," said Mabel. "Ve vill play chess again, and I vill drink your blood like a vampire. If I bite you, then you become a vampire. Vampires love company. They vant to control the vorld by making everyvone into a vampire." Mabel bared her teeth and led Robert out of the room.

"Sam," wailed Robert. "I don't want to play chess with a vampire."

"Tell somebody who cares," muttered Sam. "Sorry about the interruption," Sam typed.

"It's okay," typed Vlad. "Actually, it's a pretty funny joke. I'll tell it to my little sister.

I bet she never heard it before, and she's a little nutty."

"Let's hope my cousin Mabel and your little sister never get together," typed in Sam.

2

THE HOUDINI OF
ROMANIA

The next weekend Mabel and her parents came for Sunday brunch. Mr. Winston, the man Sam and Robert's mother was dating, was there, too. He had brought the bagels, cream cheese, and pink lox, or smoked salmon. He brought a couple of extra onion and garlic bagels because he knew they were Sam's favorite. He knew that Sam and Robert didn't love lox; he had also brought salami.

"I'll have salami, too," said Mabel, who on this day was dressed all in pink. "Did you know that in Romania they often have a sausage called *patriciani* for breakfast? But Vlad doesn't like them. He hates to get up in the morning. Nadia says he is very lazy."

"We think it's wonderful that Sam encouraged Mabel to have a friend in Romania," said Mabel's mother. "She's learning so much." Mabel's parents thought everything Mabel did was special.

"I don't think everything about the Web is good," said Mrs. Bamford. "That's why I moved the computer into the living room, so I can watch what the boys are doing. Still, I do think it's great that Sam gets to play chess with a boy from Romania."

"Did you know that the real Count Dracula's name was Vlad?" said Mabel. "I found that out on the Web."

"Maybe the Vlad you're playing chess with is a vampire," said Robert.

"My friend Vlad is not a vampire," said Sam.

"Well, Nadia says Vlad can be very mean," said Mabel, "and vampires are mean."

"Some people think that vampires are just creatures of the night who are misunderstood," teased Mr. Winston.

"Maybe Vlad doesn't like sausage for

breakfast because he only drinks blood," said Mabel. "Nadia says—"

"Will you stop starting every sentence with 'Nadia says'?" complained Sam. "I should never have let you start e-mailing Vlad's little sister. He says she can be a pest—just like two people at this table."

"Hey, I didn't do anything," argued Robert.

Mabel ignored them both. "Nadia says once he put a carp in her bed," she blurted out.

"What's a carp?" asked Robert.

"I'm not sure," admitted Mabel. It was one of the rare times that she didn't know something. "Nadia said it was smelly. I meant to ask her what it was, but I forgot."

"It's a type of fish," said Mr. Winston. "People in eastern Europe like to have it for Christmas. They often keep carps in their bathtubs around Christmastime."

"Yuck," said Robert.

"Nadia says the real Count Dracula's castle is right in Bucharest in the neighborhood where Vlad and Nadia live," added Mabel. "She told me the original Count Dracula was called Vlad the Impaler, because he liked to drive stakes through his enemies and impale them."

"Be careful, Sam," said Robert. "If you ever beat Vlad at chess, he might impale you on a stake."

"Nadia says that sometimes Vlad the Impaler wouldn't just put heads on a stake. He would put someone's foot on a spike and twist it. That's one way to impale someone—"

"Mabel, dear," said Mrs. Bamford gently, "I think we've heard enough about impaling during a meal."

"Yeah," said Sam, pretending he had a stake in his heart. "The only impaling my Vlad does is when he beats me at chess."

"Sam," said Mr. Winston, taking a bite of salami, "maybe one day you or your friend from Romania will be as good as Buddy Ryan. Did you know that Buddy Ryan is playing at the Empire Tournament in New York in just a couple of weeks? It's a two-day event. I'll try to get you tickets."

"That would be fantastic," exclaimed Sam. "Vlad will be so jealous when he finds out I'm going. You know, Vlad is just a beginner, but he's really, really good."

"I don't see why he plays with you," said Robert sullenly. "Unless he likes drinking your blood." (He was still jealous of all the time Sam spent on-line with Vlad.)

"He doesn't drink my blood," said Sam. "Stop being silly."

"You know," said Mabel, "Nadia says Vlad spends all his time inside playing chess. If he were a real vampire he couldn't go out in the daylight."

"You did say that he didn't like breakfast," Robert reminded her.

"I bet real vampires don't like breakfast," said Mabel.

"Take your vampire talk someplace else," insisted Sam. "Vlad and I have a date to play."

"What time is it in Romania?" asked Robert.

Mabel counted on her fingers. "It's seven hours later. It's almost ten o'clock in Romania."

"Wow, he's allowed to stay up late," said Robert.

"Well, he's older," said Sam. "He's twelve. Maybe kids in Romania can stay up later."

"Nadia can't," said Mabel. "Nadia told me we can only instant message on weekends. During the week, she's asleep by nine. But she did say her older brother hardly slept. And Dracula didn't sleep at night, either," Mabel added.

"I told you—cut it out," snapped Sam. "Vlad's not a vampire. I'm going to play chess."

"Come on, Robert and Mabel," said Mrs. Bamford. "Why don't you watch a video and leave Sam alone?"

"Thanks, Mom," said Sam gratefully. He went to the computer. There was already an instant message flashing from Vlad. "Are you ready? It's your turn to play the white pieces."

Sam liked to be white because he got to make the first move. He moved a pawn. The game went quickly without Sam or Vlad talking much. Sam felt good. Chess is a game of territory, and for once Sam felt he was winning. With his next move, Sam captured Vlad's remaining knight.

Thousands of miles away, Vlad slumped in front of his computer. He had actually made a mistake. He almost never made a mistake in chess—especially with Sam. Vlad studied the board, trying to picture all the possibilities and to see three or four moves ahead. This was Vlad's gift—to be able to see ahead.

Vlad could see only one desperate move to make. If he could get Sam to take his queen, then he would have a chance. Vlad moved his queen into danger.

"What's he doing?" Sam exclaimed. "I'm going to win!" he shouted. Mabel and Robert came running over from the television. Sam was actually glad to see them. He wanted them to watch him finally triumph over Vlad.

"What's going on?" asked Robert.

"I've got him!" said Sam proudly. "I'm going to get him. Watch me."

Sam gobbled up Vlad's queen. But this was exactly what Vlad had wanted. By sacrificing his queen, he had pulled Sam into a trap.

Vlad's lowly pawn was suddenly a threat to Sam's king. And now it was Sam who could not escape. Vlad won once again.

"You're the Houdini of Romania!" Sam typed.

"Houdini?" asked Vlad.

"The famous magician who could get out of straitjackets. Haven't you heard of him?" asked Sam. "He held all the secrets of magic. You should tell me the secret of why you always win."

"Maybe someday I will," typed Vlad. He chewed his lip. It was time he told his friend in America his own secret. But he was scared. Maybe his friend wouldn't like him when he found out. There was so little time. He would have to tell him soon.

Back in America, Sam wasn't even aware that Vlad had a secret. He typed in TAFN, short for "That's All For Now," and signed off.

Later that night, as they were getting ready for bed, Robert said to Sam, "Wouldn't it be funny if you really were playing chess with a vampire? I mean, you two haven't met. For all we know he has really big teeth."

"Don't be stupid," said Sam.

"Well, just to be on the safe side, why don't you ask him to send you a picture?" suggested Robert.

Sam sighed. "Okay," he said. Sam *was* curious to see what Vlad looked like. "I will."

The next day, Vlad and Sam exchanged pictures over the Internet. Sam sent a picture of himself smiling and standing on the *Alice in Wonderland* statue in Central Park. He thought Vlad would like the picture because the book *Alice in Wonderland* had a lot of chess in it.

Vlad sent Sam his class picture. His mouth was closed and he wasn't smiling. Sam studied it, trying to find his joking chess partner in the very serious picture.

3

A SMOOTH YELLOW COWARDLY LIAR

The next day, Mabel stopped Sam in the hallway at school. She was wearing all yellow. Some people look good in yellow, but not Mabel.

"You must be so excited," said Mabel.

"About what?" asked Sam. "The fact that you look like a yellow submarine?"

"No, that Vlad and Nadia are coming to America in a couple of weeks."

"What?!" shrieked Sam.

"Yes! He's coming for a chess tournament."

"That can't be. He would have told me before he told you."

"I don't think so," said Mabel smugly. "And

Vlad didn't tell me. Nadia did. Nadia says he's sneaky. She said that when he got his grand master ranking he didn't even tell her or his parents. They had to hear it from his chess teacher."

"He's not a grand master. He just started playing chess."

"Like not!" said Mabel. "He's been playing since he was five years old."

"You're lying."

"No, he's the youngest grand master chess champion Romania has ever had. He's coming here for a chess championship."

"My Vlad, a grand master . . . that can't be true. He told me that he started just about the same time I did. I know he's better than I am, but he can't be *that* much better."

"Well, it's true," Mabel insisted.

"You . . . you . . . You're a yellow bug!"

"Hey," said Mabel. "I'm just the messenger. Don't be mad at me. It's Vlad who's been lying to you."

Sam felt like exploding. If Mabel was telling the truth, she was right. He shouldn't be mad at her. He should be mad at Vlad. But that didn't help Sam's mood at all. Vlad was thousands of miles away.

After school, walking home with Robert, Sam was in an even worse mood. He wouldn't talk with Robert.

"What did I do wrong?" Robert asked him.

"Nothing. Can't I just be in a bad mood? Just don't talk to me, will you?"

"We always talk walking home from school," said Robert. "And when you're mad it's usually something I did."

"It wasn't you. It was Mabel."

"Oh," said Robert. "Well, that's more like it. It's always Mabel. What did she do today? She looked like a yellow shark. Remember that joke? What's smooth and yellow and very scary?"

"Vlad . . ." muttered Sam.

"Huh? The answer's a shark-infested custard," said Robert. "What does Vlad have to do with it?"

"He's a smooth and yellow cowardly liar," said Sam.

"Vlad! A cowardly lion, like in *The Wizard of Oz*?"

"I said 'cowardly liar,'" snapped Sam. "And just shut up about Vlad. I don't want to talk about him."

"I didn't bring him up, you did!" argued Robert. "I don't get it. I thought Vlad was your new best friend—even if he is a vampire."

"He's not a vampire. Do you not know the meaning of the words 'Shut up'?" yelled Sam.

Robert buttoned his lip, and they walked the rest of the way in silence. At home, their mother was working on the computer. "Sam, Vlad's been trying to send you an instant message for the last hour. I told him that you'd try to contact him when you got home. I'll just finish what I'm doing and you can have the computer."

"I don't want it," said Sam. He went into his room and slammed the door.

"What's wrong with Sam?" Mrs. Bamford asked.

"I'm innocent," said Robert. "I didn't do anything."

"Nobody accused you of doing anything," said Mrs. Bamford. "I was just wondering what was wrong with Sam. Usually he can't wait to be on the computer with Vlad."

"Well, today he snapped my head off when I mentioned Vlad. He's in a very bad mood."

The computer began beeping, which was the signal that there was an instant message waiting. Mrs. Bamford got up from the computer and knocked on Sam's door.

"Go away," Sam muttered.

"Sam," said Mrs. Bamford, "let me in for just a minute."

Sam got up from his bed and opened his door a crack.

"Vlad clearly wants to say something to you," said Mrs. Bamford. "He's on-line right now."

"I don't want to talk to Vlad."

"But honey, he's your friend."

"Some friend," mumbled Sam. "He's a liar."

"What?" asked Mrs. Bamford, a little alarmed. She kept close tabs on what Sam and Robert did on the computer and whom they talked to.

"It turns out that he's a much better chess

player than he said," replied Sam.

"Oh, is that all?" said Mrs. Bamford, a little relieved.

"Well, it's a big thing if you're playing chess," said Sam. "He should have told me that he's a grand master."

"Grand master?" asked Mrs. Bamford. "Is that such a big deal?"

"Such a big deal!" Sam rolled his eyes. Sometimes he forgot how little his mom knew about chess. "Almost no kids *ever* are grand masters—except Buddy Ryan. To be a grand master, you have to play in international tournaments and win all the time and get points. Vlad told me he was just a beginner, like I am. It turns out he's some chess genius."

"Sam, how did you hear all this about Vlad?"

"Mabel," admitted Sam. "Vlad's sister, Nadia, told her."

"Mabel?" asked Mrs. Bamford. "I love my niece, but honestly, Sam, you know Mabel loves to do things that annoy you. I think Vlad deserves a chance to tell his side of the story. If you're a good friend, you give the other person a chance, even if—or especially if—that person lives thousands of miles away. Maybe in Romania you're not supposed to tell anyone of your accomplishments."

"I guess you're right," said Sam reluctantly.

"Come on," said Mrs. Bamford, putting her arm around him. "Go to the computer." She laughed. "I never thought I'd ever find myself saying those words. Usually, I'm trying to get you off the computer."

Sam went out into the living room. Robert was playing a computer game, but he slipped off the chair quickly and gave the computer to Sam, something he almost never did.

Vlad's message was, "Sam, I need to tell you something."

"I heard already that you're coming to New York, grand master," typed in Sam. Then he typed ☹.

"You heard," typed Vlad.

"How could you not tell me?!"

"I knew I must," typed Vlad. "But I wasn't sure I would be able to go to the Empire Tournament. I was only picked at the last minute when another player couldn't go. Until I was sure, I didn't want to tell you. I have big nerves."

"Big nerves?" repeated Sam.

"Big nerves. . . . I will explain when we see each other. My English is not good enough. I know I lied to you. Please, tell me that you will meet with me. I want to see your New York."

Sam stared out the window. The Empire State Building's top floors, antenna, and lightning rod were shining brightly in the night sky.

"Yeah, I'll show you the Vampire State Building," wrote Sam. The words just popped into his head.

"What?" Vlad wrote.

"Nothing; it's a joke," typed Sam. "I meant the Empire State Building. It's really beautiful. My brother and my cousin think you're related to a vampire, but I told them they were just being silly."

"If only I could tell you what is in my heart. But the words do not come," wrote Vlad.

"We have an English word called 'liar,'" wrote Sam. "How do you say that in Romanian?"

"*Mincinos*," typed Vlad. "It is one of the worst things you can call somebody."

"It is in our language, too," wrote Sam.

"Please don't be too mad at me," begged Vlad. "You are my friend in America and I want to see you."

"But why did you lie to me?"

"I was afraid," typed Vlad.

"Afraid of what?"

"Please," begged Vlad. "It will be so much easier to explain when I see you. Can we not wait?"

Sam didn't type anything for a minute.

"Are you still there?" asked Vlad.

"I'm thinking. . . ." typed Sam.

"Like a chess move?" asked Vlad.

"This isn't chess," typed Sam.

"I know," typed Vlad. "You are mad at me. But when we meet I will be able to make it all clear."

"Any other lies that I don't know about?" asked Sam.

"Please . . . when we meet, I will explain it all. . . . And maybe we can still be friends. Do you think that is possible? Could you come to the airport and meet us? You are the first face I want to see in America."

"I'll have to ask my mother," wrote Sam. "I have to go now." He wanted time to think.

"So what did Vlad say?" asked Robert when Sam turned away from the computer. Sam had forgotten Robert and his mother were in the room.

"Well, he really is coming to New York. He wondered if we could meet him at the airport. He says that mine is the first face he wants to see."

"That's so sweet," said Mrs. Bamford. "Of course, we'll meet them at the airport. If you give me their address, I'll e-mail his parents."

Robert was staring out the window with his back to Sam. Sam sighed.

"I'm sorry I snapped at you," said Sam. "I was mad at Vlad, not you."

"Did he explain why he lied?" asked Robert.

"Not exactly," said Sam.

"What does he want?"

"He said he wants to see our New York." Sam looked out the window. "I told him I'd take him to the Vampire State Building."

"Because he's a vampire?" asked Robert.

"No. . . . It was a joke. I meant the Empire State Building. Vlad's not a vampire."

"Remember when we saw the old movie *King Kong*?" asked Robert. "The one where the big ape hung from the top of the Empire State Building."

"King Kong wasn't real," Sam reminded Robert. "Neither are vampires."

Robert looked up at his older brother. He sure hoped Sam was right.

4

ONCE UPON A PAWN

Over the next two weeks, Mrs. Bamford was in touch with Vlad's parents through e-mail. "They seem like such nice people," she said. It was the night before Vlad was expected to arrive, and Mr. Winston had come for supper.

"I rented a van so we can take everybody back together," said Mr. Winston.

"That's because Mabel insists on going, too," complained Sam.

"Well, she's excited to meet Nadia," said Mrs. Bamford. "I think it's nice that Vlad's little sister will have Mabel to greet her."

Sam didn't say anything. He still wasn't sure how he felt about Vlad. They hadn't played chess together since Sam had learned the truth, though they'd exchanged a few polite e-mails in which both boys claimed they were busy. The truth was Sam was afraid to play with Vlad now that he had learned how good Vlad was. And even after almost two weeks, he was still mad at Vlad for not telling him that he was a grand master.

The next day, when the Bamfords and Mr. Winston stopped to pick up Mabel, they saw she was dressed in an unusual outfit, even for her.

"You look like a checkerboard," Sam told her as she climbed into the van. She was dressed in black-and-white checked pants and a shirt with one white arm and one black arm.

"I told Nadia that's how she'd recognize me," said Mabel. "And I've got a sign." Mabel had made a computer banner that said BUN VENIT VLAD AND NADIA! ☺

"*Bun venit* is 'welcome' in Romanian," said Mabel. "I found a website of Romanian words. Here, Sam. This will help you talk to Vlad."

Mabel handed a computer printout to Sam.

"That's very nice, dear," said Mrs. Bamford. "How do you say 'thank you' in Romanian?"

"Mult'umese," said Mabel.

Sam scowled. He didn't feel like saying thank you, or anything else, to Vlad.

"Do you think Vlad will have fangs?" asked Robert.

"What?" asked Sam.

"Well, if he's a vampire, he might," said Robert.

"He's not a vampire. He's a liar."

"I bet real vampires lie all the time," said Robert.

"Oh, please," said Sam, shaking his head. When they got to the airport, they parked and went into the international arrivals terminal. Mrs. Bamford made them all stay together so they didn't get lost.

Sam watched the faces of the people coming out of customs. Then he recognized Vlad from the picture he'd sent. His brown hair was a little longer, and he was dressed in jeans and a jean jacket. Next to him was a little girl dressed all in black and white.

"Nadia!" screeched Mabel. "I'm Mabel. It's me!"

Nadia started jumping up and down and waving. Vlad shook his head, looking annoyed. Behind them were two adults who looked much more exhausted than the kids.

Mrs. Bamford smiled at them. She held out her hand. "Mr. and Mrs. Clinciu, welcome. This is my friend Mr. Winston. And my sons, Sam and Robert. My niece Mabel has already bonded with Nadia. We're all so excited to meet you."

Sam looked anything but excited. Robert went to talk to Mabel and Nadia. While the adults chatted, Vlad and Sam stood awkwardly in front of each other. Vlad tried to smile. His teeth were crooked. Sam thought Vlad's eyes seemed a little sad.

"Sam?" Vlad asked. The *s* came out more like a *z*.

Vlad smiled. Robert was staring at him. Not only were Vlad's teeth crooked, but also his two incisors were pointy.

Vlad reached out his arms and moved toward Sam.

"Yikes!" squeaked Robert.

Sam jumped.

Vlad blinked. "I'm sorry," he said quickly. "In our country, it is a custom to hug friends when we meet."

"It's all right, Vlad," said Mr. Winston. "In our country boys don't hug as much, but I think it's a nice custom." He gave Vlad a hug.

Sam held out his hand to Vlad.

Vlad shook his hand.

"I'm glad he didn't hug you," whispered Robert to Sam as they walked to the baggage claim.

"Why?" asked Sam.

"Because his teeth look like a vampire's teeth."

"Shh," said Sam.

"Well, they do," said Robert. "I'll have to tell Mabel."

The baggage claim area was so crowded that Sam and Vlad didn't really have time to talk. Once they got into the van, Mabel and Nadia sat squished in the middle next to Mr.

and Mrs. Clinciu. Sam, Vlad, and Robert sat in the backseat.

"I like being with you," said Nadia in English to Mabel. "I don't want to sit in the back with my brother. He did nothing but play chess on his computer the whole flight."

Vlad whispered something to Nadia in Romanian.

"What did he say?" asked Mabel.

"He said we look like checkerboards—and he doesn't play checkers," said Nadia.

"That's pretty funny," admitted Sam. Nadia and Mabel did look like twin checkerboards.

"Sam," said Vlad, "I must try to explain why I didn't tell you I was a grand master. Everyone I play always thinks I am so special. But you didn't. You just liked playing chess. And you were funny."

"I'm funnier than he is," said Robert. "He gets all his jokes from me. Do you know how chess players start bedtime stories?"

"No," said Vlad.

"One pawn at a time . . ."

"Hey," said Mabel. "I told you that joke."

"But I told it better," said Robert.

"Jokes in English are hard to understand," Vlad said.

"Once upon a time . . . one pawn at a time . . . Do you get it now?" asked Robert.

Vlad ignored him. He turned and whispered to Sam, "Do you forgive me for not telling you? I want us to be friends."

"I guess maybe if I were a genius at chess I wouldn't want everybody to know," admitted Sam quietly.

"I knew you'd understand," said Vlad.

"Look, Nadia," said Mabel. "See that pretty building right in front of us? The one that's all lit up? That's the Empire State Building."

"The Vampire State Building, right, Vlad?" joked Robert, nudging him with his elbow.

"What?" asked Vlad, looking a little alarmed.

"It was a joke," said Sam.

"Why are the lights on the top green and gold?" asked Nadia's mother.

"It's for India's Independence Day," explained Mrs. Bamford. "The lights that shine on the Empire State Building change colors for different occasions."

"I know," said Vlad's father. "Perhaps if Vlad wins the chess tournament, they will light the building in blue, yellow, and red—the colors of the Romanian flag. It would be a great honor."

Vlad looked glum. "Nobody's going to beat Buddy Ryan," he said.

"Don't you want to win for your country's honor?" asked Sam. "Everyone can see the Empire State Building for miles around. The whole world will know if you win."

"I don't want the world to know a lot more about me," said Vlad.

"What does that mean?" asked Sam.

Vlad shook his head. "I can't tell you right now," he whispered.

"Not more secrets," said Sam.

"I know you are my friend," said Vlad. "But if I told you this one, even you might not want to be my friend."

Sam thought about it. What other secrets did Vlad have?

"You must be so tired," said Mrs. Bamford

as they dropped off Vlad's family at their hotel. "Tomorrow we'd love to have you all to our house for dinner."

"You are so kind," said Mrs. Clinciu.

Next they dropped off Mabel.

"Everybody to bed," said Mrs. Bamford when they got home. "It's been a long day. And we need rest almost as much as Vlad does."

"Can I just check the computer?" Sam asked, more out of habit than from thinking he had any important messages. But when Sam logged on, there was a message from Vlad.

"I am so thankful to have met you in person," Vlad had written. "I am very nervous. I don't think I will sleep at all in New York."

Sam was puzzled. Vlad should have been sleepy from jet lag. He e-mailed back, "You will be fine. I think you should go to sleep. Here's a bedtime story: Once upon a pawn, a boy named Vlad came from Romania and slew all his opponents. His knights were unstoppable. His queen was all-powerful.

His king never died. Sleep tight. Sam."

Suddenly there was an instant message from Vlad.

"Thank you," wrote Vlad. "You are my true friend."

"Sam," said Mrs. Bamford, looking over Sam's shoulder, "tell Vlad that he has to go to sleep and so do you."

"My mom says you should go to sleep," Sam typed. Then he added, "GTG," which stood for "got to go." Sam signed off.

After Sam had turned off the computer, Mrs. Bamford asked, "Did you find out why Vlad didn't tell you he was a grand master?"

"He said he had fun playing with me. I think it bugged him that everyone always treated him like he was so special. But then . . . Mom, he said he had another secret."

Mrs. Bamford looked concerned. "Well, some secrets are all right to keep, but if something is worrying him, he should be able to tell someone. And if something he tells you worries you, you can tell me, and we'll work out what's best together. Okay?"

Sam nodded. Sometimes his mom really

made him feel better. Sam went to get ready for bed. When he got to the bathroom, Robert was already there, staring at his teeth in the bathroom mirror.

"My teeth are straight," said Robert. "Did you notice something funny about Vlad's and Nadia's teeth? They were crooked."

"So maybe they don't have a great dentist. Maybe that's a problem in Romania. Stop hogging the sink," said Sam.

"Mabel *was* right about one thing," said Robert. "The real Count Dracula *did* come from Romania."

"There are no real Romanian vampires," said Sam. "That's just a myth."

"You're wrong," said Robert. "I looked it up on the Web. Ask Vlad."

"He's got a lot on his mind," said Sam. "I don't think he needs any questions about vampires. He's having trouble sleeping."

"You know vampires don't sleep at night," said Robert.

"Well, I do," said Sam. "I'm going to bed." And he did.

While Sam went straight to sleep, Robert

found that his mind was still racing. Mabel had said that vampires were real—and many of them came from Romania. What if Vlad just happened to be a Romanian vampire? If he was, then this vampire was in Robert's hometown, just a few blocks away.

5

IF A VAMPIRE EATS GARLIC, IT SHRIVELS UP

The next night Mabel and her parents and the Clincius came over to the Bamfords' apartment.

"We had a wonderful day," said Mrs. Clinciu. "Vlad practiced a little, but then we walked all over. We saw Rockefeller Center."

"We had hot dogs," said Nadia.

"Now you'll try another New York traditional food," said Mrs. Bamford. "We're going to order Chinese food. Why don't you look at the menu? We want to get dishes that you like."

"Oh, we eat anything," said Mr. Clinciu. "Just not too much garlic. For some reason, everyone in our family is allergic to garlic."

Mabel's eyes widened. "Did you hear that?" she whispered to Robert and Sam.

"Yeah, no shredded pork with garlic sauce—it's one of my favorites," said Sam.

"Don't you know that all vampires are allergic to garlic?" whispered Mabel.

"What's going on?" asked Vlad.

"I was just saying that if vampires eat garlic they die," said Mabel.

"Vampires?" asked Vlad. He looked a little tense.

"Yes," said Mabel. "I read that if vampires eat garlic they shrivel up and die."

"Shrivel?" asked Nadia, not understanding the word.

Mabel demonstrated by shaking dramatically all over and falling to the floor in a heap. Nadia stared at her and started giggling.

"You look like Vlad when he gets nervous before a tournament," said Nadia.

"Vlad, are you nervous?" asked Sam.

"Yes. Very," admitted Vlad.

Meanwhile, Mabel's mother was alarmed

that her daughter was still sprawled on the floor.

"Mabel?" asked her mother. "Are you all right?"

"I'm just demonstrating what happens when some people eat garlic," said Mabel from the floor.

There was an awkward silence.

"A lot of people are allergic to garlic," said Mrs. Bamford. "Kids, why don't you go play. We'll order the food."

"Nadia," said Mabel, "I brought you a present. It's one of my Barbie dolls, and I have lots of matching outfits for her."

"Ohhhh . . . I love Barbie," gushed Nadia.

Sam took Vlad over to his computer. Robert felt left out. He certainly didn't want to play with Nadia, Mabel, and the Barbie doll, but Vlad and Sam were talking chess.

"Hey, Vlad?" asked Robert. "Do you want to see my gerbils? One's alive and one's stuffed."

"Stuffed?" asked Vlad, sure he had misunderstood an English word again.

"Yeah," said Robert. "He died, and Sam had him stuffed for me so I'd always remember him."

"Is that an American tradition?" asked Vlad.

"Uh . . . no," said Sam. "It's kind of a tradition I started."

"Personally," said Mrs. Bamford, "I am hoping it will be a one-of-a-kind event. Go on, kids. We'll call you when the food comes."

In Robert's room, Vlad admired Robert's surviving gerbil, Terminator, and the lifelike stuffed gerbil, Exterminator. Nadia and Mabel soon followed them. Nadia squealed when she saw the stuffed gerbil.

Vlad wandered over to the chessboard and picked up the black knight. "The knight is my favorite attack piece," he said, fingering it slowly. "I just hope tomorrow my knight will do my bidding. They are making me play in the morning. In the daylight," he complained. "I wish they held the tournament at night."

"Knights . . . nights," muttered Sam.

"Vlad, you sure like nights."

"Is that a joke? Jokes are hard in English," said Vlad.

"But your English is so good," said Sam.

Vlad shook his head. "I wish you could speak Romanian. There is so much in my heart that I can't tell you."

Vlad looked out the window. Sam joined him. The moon was almost full and was right in the center of the New York skyline. The Empire State Building lights were white.

"New York really is beautiful," said Vlad.

"I know," said Sam. "I love New York."

"Me, too," said Vlad. "And I love having a friend here. You are my friend, aren't you?"

Sam nodded. "You know, my mom says there are some secrets that shouldn't be kept. If it's something I can help you with, you can trust me—or my mom. She'll help."

"Nobody can help me," said Vlad. "It is a family curse. . . ."

"A family curse . . . You mean like being allergic to garlic?" Robert blurted out. Sam gave him a dirty look. He'd forgotten that Robert, Nadia, and Mabel were in the room.

50

Sam felt that Vlad was very close to telling him his secret, and he was sure it had nothing to do with garlic.

"No, this isn't like being allergic. We have big nerves . . . in our family," said Vlad.

"Big nerves?" asked Sam. "Is that your secret?"

Vlad shook his head.

"You mean bigger nerves than other humans?" asked Robert.

"I guess so," said Vlad, sounding confused. "Maybe that's not exactly what I mean."

"Hey, kids," shouted Mrs. Bamford. "Come on. The food's here. And no garlic."

Vlad clapped his hand on Sam's shoulder. "I shouldn't bother you with my problems," he said.

He turned to Nadia, Mabel, and Robert. "Come on, let's eat."

"What happens to people in your family when they eat garlic?" Robert asked Nadia.

"Ohhh, it's disgusting," said Nadia. "You don't want to know."

6

A DRAGON WITH BAD BREATH

On Saturday, Mabel's parents dropped her off at the Bamfords' so she could go to the chess tournament with them. Mabel was dressed yet again in black and white. This time, she wore pants with one black leg and one white leg.

"Wherever did you find those?" asked Mrs. Bamford.

"It wasn't easy," muttered Mabel's mother. "But you know Mabel."

"I think every thrift shop in New York City knows Mabel," said Mrs. Bamford. She told Sam and Robert to get their coats. They took the subway to the tournament, which was being held in a building right across the street from the Empire State Building.

"This building used to be a department store," said Mrs. Bamford.

"I think that's a good sign," said Mabel as they went into the lobby.

"Why?" asked Sam. "Vlad doesn't like to shop."

"No, but I do," said Mabel.

"You think the world revolves around you," said Sam.

"No, I don't," said Mabel, sounding genuinely hurt.

"I'm sorry," Sam muttered.

Mabel stared at him. It wasn't like Sam to apologize. He was nervous, almost as if he, not Vlad, were going to have to play in the tournament.

"It's okay," said Mabel. "Oh! There they are!" Mabel spotted Nadia, Vlad, and their parents. Nadia and Mr. and Mrs. Clinciu looked rested, but Vlad looked pale and tired.

"*Bună Dimeneata!*" Mabel shouted out. "That's 'good morning' in Romanian," she explained to Sam and Robert.

Nadia ran to Mabel and hugged her. Mrs. Bamford and Mr. Winston hugged Mr. and Mrs. Clinciu. Only Vlad stood apart, looking very nervous. He didn't try to hug Sam.

"Hi," said Sam. "I mean, *Bună ziua*. Doesn't that mean 'hello'?"

Vlad shook Sam's hand. "Thank you for learning a little Romanian," he said.

"That's the only Romanian I know," said Sam. "Mabel's learned a lot more."

"But she isn't my good luck charm," said Vlad. "You are."

"Come on, Vlad," said Mr. Clinciu. "Let's go."

Sam and Vlad followed the adults into the main room on the first floor. Mabel, Nadia, and Robert were behind them. There was a large mirror covering one whole wall from when the building was a department store.

Vlad quickly turned his face away from the mirror, tripping over Sam.

"You okay, buddy?" asked Sam.

"Yeah," said Vlad. Then Vlad's father called him over to sign some papers.

Mabel poked Robert with her elbow.

"Ouch," said Robert.

"Did you see that?"

"What?" asked Robert.

"Vlad didn't want to look at himself in the mirror. I think that's something that vampires are afraid of."

"What are you talking about?" Sam asked.

"Vampires can't see themselves in a mirror," said Mabel, preening at her own image.

"Well, I guess you're not a vampire," said Sam. "You like to look at yourself in the mirror."

"I'm not a vampire," said Mabel. "But maybe Vlad really is one."

"You've got vampires on the brain," said Sam. "This is a chess tournament, not a movie theater. And vampires only exist in movies and books. They aren't real."

"Sam just doesn't want to hear the truth," Mabel complained to Robert.

Robert nodded. He was surprised that he agreed with Mabel. It was a little weird.

They caught up to Vlad and his parents. The main hall was crowded. Reporters and photographers were everywhere, all of them there to interview Buddy Ryan. The teenage chess star was giving a press conference, which was being broadcast on a big screen. He had freckles and a very open face.

Sam saw Vlad staring at the big screen. Buddy Ryan looked amazingly relaxed. "What do you make of the news that the Empire State Building will go red, white, and blue when you win this tournament?" asked one reporter.

"Well, first I have to win," said Buddy modestly. "There are a lot of good players here from all around the world."

"That's you," whispered Sam to Vlad. "You're really good."

"Not as good as him," said Vlad. "Come on. I've seen enough."

Sam and Vlad made their way through the hall. Chessboards were lying on the carpets like a crazy black-and-white maze. Practice games between players and coaches were in progress everywhere.

Vlad's father found a corner for them all to sit. He took out a portable chess set. "Vlad, do you want to play a quick game with Sam to warm up?" he asked.

Vlad shook his head.

"Come on," said Sam. "You know you'll win. You always beat me."

"I don't think so. Not today," said Vlad. Vlad's eyes were bloodshot, and he looked very tired.

"Are you okay?" Sam asked him worriedly.

Vlad shook his head. "I couldn't sleep," he said. "I don't think I will win."

"Hey," said Sam. "Of course you'll win. You're fierce."

"I'm not so fierce," said Vlad.

"Vlad, don't go soft on me now," said Sam. "I'm rooting for you. I want you to be as fierce as when you trap me."

Vlad took a deep breath. The bell rang for the contestants to move into the big room where the tournament would be played.

Vlad gave them all one sad look as he walked into the room. "He doesn't look good," said Mabel.

"He's just tired," said Sam.

Mrs. Bamford, Mr. Winston, Sam, Robert,

and Mabel made their way to the balcony. The Clincius were sitting in a separate section for family on the main floor.

Up in the balcony, the Bamfords and Mabel could look down at the chessboards arranged in long rows in the large room. The black and white squares were dizzying.

Vlad's first opponent was a young woman with long hair and bangs. She and Vlad shook hands. Neither smiled. Vlad was pale, but the woman became even paler as Vlad won in just eight moves.

Vlad looked up at the balcony and gave Sam a big grin. After his win, he didn't look quite so ghostly. His crooked incisors seemed to gleam. Then he went on to his next game, which he won, and then the next.

"Do you notice that Vlad's opponents get very pale when he plays them?" Mabel whispered to Sam and Robert.

"So what?" said Sam.

"Well, when a vampire drinks a person's blood the person becomes pale," said Mabel. "It's a fact."

"Will you stop yammering," said Sam. He

wanted to follow the action down on the floor.

Vlad ploughed through his opponents, mowing them down one after another.

"Wow!" said Robert, finally paying attention. "There aren't many left."

"He's in the final four!" exclaimed Sam excitedly.

The bell rang, signaling the end of the day's matches. Mabel, Sam, and Robert made their way down from the balcony to congratulate Vlad.

Mrs. Bamford went up to Vlad's parents and gave them each a hug. "Congratulations, Vlad," said Mrs. Bamford, putting her arms around him.

Vlad looked a little embarrassed by the hug.

"Hey, you won," said Sam. "You said that you couldn't and you did. I think you can win it all. Tomorrow I bet you will beat Buddy Ryan in the finals."

"No . . . I could never beat Buddy Ryan, I don't think," said Vlad.

"Sure you can," said Sam. "When Buddy Ryan plays you, he'll find he's playing a dragon."

"Me a dragon?" said Vlad. "I like that idea."

"Yes, the dragon of the tournament," said Sam.

Mrs. Bamford turned to the whole group. "I have a treat for everybody. Mr. Winston has gotten us all tickets for a tour of the Empire State Building across the street. We don't even have to stand in line."

"We are going to the Empire State Building?" asked Vlad. "You told me that one day you would take me there," Vlad said to Sam.

"Yeah." Sam laughed. "Except I called it the Vampire State Building. But there are no vampires there."

"What are you talking about?" Nadia asked Mabel.

"Your brother," said Mabel. "Sam just called him a dragon."

Nadia's eyes went wide.

"What's wrong?" Mabel asked.

"*Dracula* comes from a Romanian word for 'dragon,'" whispered Nadia. "But don't tell Vlad I told you that."

"Why?" asked Mabel. "Does he breathe fire?"

"He does have very bad breath," said Nadia, "even though he doesn't eat garlic."

"Maybe he ate some garlic by mistake," said Mabel, nudging Robert, whose rib cage was getting a little sore from all of Mabel's nudging.

"Come on," said Mrs. Bamford. "Let's get going."

As they headed for the Empire State Building, Vlad had his arm around Sam's shoulders. Robert looked at his brother. Was he in the clutches of a vampire? Could Sam really be in danger and not know it? If so, Robert knew it was up to him to save Sam. But how?

THAT'S THE WAY THE PIGEON POOPS

The marble lobby of the Empire State Building was crowded. First everyone stood in line to go through the metal detectors and security guards. Vlad, Nadia, and their parents stared at the tourists from all over the world. People were speaking many different languages—English, Korean, French, Hindi, and Russian.

Once they were through security, they walked past the massive stained-glass panels in the lobby. The panels showed the seven wonders of the ancient world, with the Empire State Building as the eighth wonder.

"Stay together," shouted Mrs. Bamford.

They got onto the high speed escalators which took them up to the second floor. There they waited for the elevators to take them to the eightieth floor. The walls were hung with historic pictures of the Empire State Building.

"Where's King Kong?" asked Nadia, looking around. "Mabel said there was a big ape."

"King Kong isn't real," said Vlad.

"Yes, he is. . . . Isn't he, Mabel?" insisted Nadia.

"No, he's not," teased Vlad. "King Kong is no more real than vampires."

"Vampires can be real," said Robert.

"So are dragons with bad breath," added Nadia.

Vlad gave her a funny look. "What do you mean?" he asked suspiciously.

Before Nadia could answer, Mabel began spouting from her guidebook. She turned to the group as if she were their self-appointed leader. "Did you know there are six thousand, five hundred windows in this building, and the building weighs three hundred sixty-five thousand tons?"

"Did you know that there's such a thing as too many facts?" said Sam.

Vlad giggled.

"I think Mabel's facts are very interesting," said Nadia. "Everything Mabel does is very interesting. And I love the way she dresses."

"That's because the two of you know only one way to dress," said Vlad.

"Bad!" said Sam and Vlad in unison. They gave each other a high five.

"Forget them, Nadia," said Mabel. "Stick with me."

The elevator doors opened. They all got in. The elevator whisked them up to the eightieth floor in a little over a minute. They all felt their ears pop as they rose higher and higher. Then they got into another elevator which took them to the eighty-sixth floor.

The observation deck seemed much bigger than it looked from the street level. There was plenty of room to move around and even to stand near the fence and look down. They could see clear across the Hudson River to New Jersey, and to the south they could see the Statue of Liberty and the place where the

World Trade Center buildings had once stood. When they looked north, all of Central Park was laid out in front of them, and they could see Yankee Stadium, way up in the Bronx.

Vlad and Nadia stared out at the city. "New York is so much prettier than I thought," Vlad said in awe.

Sam looked out. He loved his city, even though he didn't always think of it as pretty. But framed by two rivers, and gleaming in the late afternoon light, it really did look beautiful. Sam was proud to show it to his friend.

"I'm glad you like it, Vlad," said Sam.

"Me, too," said Vlad. "Do you really forgive me for lying to you about being a grand master?"

"Yeah," said Sam. "I guess I can understand that you wouldn't want everyone to know. And besides, now that I've seen you play, I'm really rooting for you."

"Is Bucharest beautiful?" asked Robert.

Vlad nodded. "Yes. It's much older and smaller than New York City. It's beautiful in a different way."

"What does Dracula's castle look like?" asked Mabel.

Sam gave her a dirty look.

"Well, he lived in Bucharest for only a little while," said Vlad. "Mostly he stayed in Sighisoara, in the country."

Vlad turned to Sam. "I want to take pictures of New York to show my classmates. Let's walk around."

"Sure," said Sam. He ran to one of the telescopes and put in enough money for fifteen minutes of viewing. "Come on. Vlad. I bet I can show you my apartment."

"First I want to take some pictures," said Vlad.

"I'll look," said Robert, and he grabbed the telescope from Sam. He pushed Sam's arm, forcing the telescope around.

Robert found he was looking through the telescope at Vlad, now much bigger than life. Magnified one hundred times, Vlad's teeth looked even more crooked, especially his two pointy incisors.

Vlad was stalking a pigeon that was on

67

one of the parapets, just outside the fence. A cloud passed overhead, covering the sun. In the shadows, Vlad's teeth looked even sharper. He drew ever closer to the pigeon. Robert's eyes widened. He handed the telescope to Sam.

"Does Vlad look funny to you?" Robert asked as Sam peered through the telescope.

"Well, he looks very interested in that pigeon," said Sam, shrugging his shoulders.

"What's going on?" asked Mabel. "Let me have the telescope. I want to show Nadia the good stores. She's just gone to the bathroom with her mother, but she'll be right out."

Mabel looked through the telescope. "Why is Vlad trying to get so close to that pigeon?" she asked.

"You should see his teeth through the telescope," said Robert. "They look huge."

"Did you know," whispered Mabel, "that vampires sometimes eat small birds when they can't get other prey?"

"Did you know," snapped Sam, "that I've had just about enough of you saying Vlad is a vampire?"

"But what if he is?" said Robert. "You know, Mabel is sometimes right about things."

"You think Mabel's right, little brother?" Sam smiled at Robert indulgently.

"Well," said Mabel, "let's count up the clues.

"Number one—he's from Romania, home of vampires.

"Number two—he doesn't like to play chess during the day.

"Number three—he's got pointy teeth.

"Number four—everybody who plays chess with him ends up looking as if someone drank their blood."

"And he stalks pigeons," added Robert.

"And tells lies," added Mabel.

Sam couldn't stand it anymore. He turned away from his brother and cousin in disgust. "Hey, Vlad!" he shouted, running over to Vlad. "What are you doing?"

Vlad looked startled. "I was looking at the bird," he said.

"It's just a pigeon," said Sam. "You looked like you thought that pigeon was the most interesting thing in all of New York City."

"Ask him if he wanted to eat it," Robert whispered into Sam's ear. He and Mabel had followed Sam.

"No," said Sam. "I'm not going to ask him that."

"Maybe they eat pigeons in Romania," said Robert reasonably.

"He wasn't going to eat that pigeon," whispered Sam.

Vlad waved his camera. "I want to get a picture of the pigeon . . . doing . . ." He couldn't come up with the word.

"What?" asked Sam. "Tell me. Does this have anything to do with the big secret?"

Vlad's eyes widened. "I can't talk about that . . . but . . . but . . ."

"Why?" asked Sam. "I think I've been a good friend. I think I deserve to know."

"Look, look!" said Vlad excitedly. "It's doing it. . . . How do you say that in English?"

Sam stared at the pigeon. It was pooping. "Poop!" exclaimed Sam. "The pigeon's pooping . . . going to the bathroom . . . only pigeons don't use bathrooms. They do it everywhere!"

Vlad's smile widened. "Exactly—just like

pigeons in Romania . . . I will take a picture so my classmates will see that New York is not so different from Bucharest."

Vlad was so eager to get the picture of the pigeon pooping that he lunged forward. As he did, he bumped into Sam. Vlad fell off balance, trying to hold on to his camera. His feet slipped out from under him and his head crashed into Sam's arm and shoulder.

Robert screamed! It looked as if Vlad was biting Sam. In fact, that's actually what happened. Sam stared at his arm as the others stared at Sam. The skin wasn't punctured, but there were definite teeth marks.

"I . . . I'm sorry," said Vlad. "I was just trying to get the pigeon pooping. I think I got it."

"Got what?" asked Robert suspiciously. He wondered if Vlad meant that he had gotten Sam to be a vampire.

Sam laughed. "Well, if you got the picture, it's worth it!" he said.

Mabel and Robert were still staring at Sam. "Sam just got bitten by a vampire," whispered Mabel. "This is scary."

Robert nodded. He couldn't believe that once again he was agreeing with Mabel. Maybe that's what happened when your brother turned into a vampire in front of your eyes.

IF YOUR BROTHER WON'T BRUSH HIS TEETH, DOES THAT MEAN HE'S A VAMPIRE?

After the visit to the Empire State Building, Vlad's family took a cab back to their hotel for the night. On the subway ride home, Robert sat next to Mabel.

"Did you see . . . Vlad's teeth?" said Robert.

"I did," whispered Mabel. "They're dangerous."

"They landed right on Sam's arm," said Robert. "They left teeth marks."

"Sam could be turning into a vampire right before our eyes," whispered Mabel. She and Robert turned to stare at Sam.

"What are you two looking at?" Sam asked,

but he had a potato chip caught in his throat, and as he spoke he coughed.

"What's wrong, honey?" asked Mrs. Bamford. "That sounded like a growl."

"Potato chip," said Sam. He coughed again and tried to clear his throat.

"Maybe that's the noise a human makes when he's turning into a vampire," whispered Mabel.

Robert's eyes widened.

"You're going to have to watch him all night," said Mabel. "That's when the teeth marks will do their damage."

"What if I can't stay up all night?" asked Robert.

"It's your duty," said Mabel.

"What are you two whispering about?" Sam asked.

"Nothing," said Robert as they reached Mabel's stop. They all got off and walked Mabel to her door. Mabel turned to Robert. "Remember, do your duty. . . ."

When Sam and Robert and their mother got home, Robert followed Sam so closely that Sam practically tripped over him.

"Give me some space, will you?" asked Sam. "What *was* Mabel yammering about?" he added, absentmindedly rubbing his arm.

"Oh, she was just figuring out her outfit for tomorrow," said Robert.

"Now you're talking outfits with Mabel! Next are you going to dress alike? Matching outfits. That'll be cute." Sam yawned.

"Are you sleepy?" asked Mrs. Bamford.

"Yeah," said Sam. "I'm beat. It was hard concentrating on all that chess. Good night, Mom." Sam kissed her good night.

Robert followed Sam into Sam's bedroom. "Are you really sleepy?" Robert asked worriedly.

"Yeah. I'm going to sleep so well I bet I wake up tomorrow a new guy," said Sam, stretching.

"A new guy or a vampire?" Robert muttered to himself.

"What are you talking about?" asked Sam, giving another huge yawn.

Robert tried to look inside his brother's mouth to see if his incisors had grown.

"Aren't you going to brush your teeth?" Robert asked.

Sam shook his head. "Don't tell Mom, I'm too tired." He lay down on the bed.

"Too tired . . ." muttered Robert. "Or are you afraid to look in the mirror?"

"What are you talking about?" Sam asked again. His little brother was annoying him. He yawned again and turned away from Robert.

Robert stared at his brother and then looked out the window. The moon was full, and in New York, only the full moon was bright enough to compete with all the lights. Robert wondered if a full moon made it easier for someone to turn into a vampire.

Robert sat on the edge of Sam's bed. He couldn't believe Sam could sleep so soundly the night after being bitten by a vampire. Robert started humming to keep himself awake. It was his duty to watch over his brother.

Sam rolled over. "Will you be quiet?" he muttered. He put the covers over his face.

Robert swallowed hard. How was he going

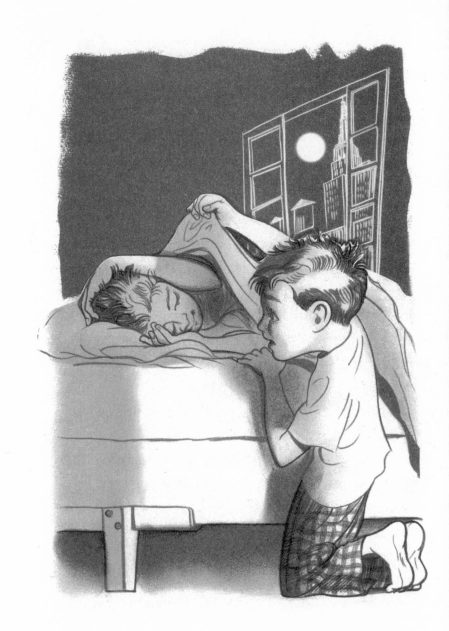

to watch his brother turn into a vampire if he was under the covers?

Robert tiptoed over and lifted the corner of Sam's blanket.

"Go away!" snapped Sam. His teeth shone briefly in the moonlight. He rolled away from Robert.

"Sam," whispered Robert.

"What?" asked Sam.

"Do you ever worry that Vlad might be . . . you know . . ."

"You know what?"

"A vampire," whispered Robert.

"Will you get out of here? Vlad is not a vampire."

"He bit you. Do you feel funny?" he asked.

"I feel sleepy!" insisted Sam. "And if you don't stop talking to me, I'm going to stuff this pillow down your throat."

"That sounds like something that Vlad the Impaler might do. . . . Are you sure you don't feel funny?"

"I'm going to impale you . . . if you don't let me sleep," complained Sam.

Within seconds, Robert heard steady breathing and little snorts, the sounds Sam usually made when he was asleep.

Robert rubbed his eyes. He tried to stay awake, but the next thing he knew their mother was waking them up. Robert jumped. Sam's face was still covered.

Mrs. Bamford shook him. "Come on, Sam . . . wake up," she said.

Robert watched as his brother slowly pulled the covers away from his face. Was he a vampire?

Sam squinched his eyes up tight and grimaced. "Five more minutes, Mom," he begged. He rolled over, pulling the covers with him.

"It's the tournament finals," said Mrs. Bamford.

"Does Sam look funny, Mom?" Robert asked.

"He always looks like a funny bunny in the morning," said Mrs. Bamford, rubbing Sam's hair.

"Yeah," muttered Robert. "A funny bunny with fangs."

"Is Robert still talking about vampires?" asked Sam from under the covers. "I'm sick of the whole subject."

Sam rolled out of bed, went into the bathroom, and slammed the door.

"Did you see, Mom?" Robert asked. "Anything different about his teeth? Do they look crooked like Vlad's?"

"Robert," warned Mrs. Bamford, "Mrs. Clinciu told me that she admires your straight teeth. They don't have many dentists in Romania who can fit children with braces. It really isn't polite to Vlad and his family to keep pointing out that Vlad has crooked teeth. I think you should drop the whole subject."

Just then the phone rang. It was Mabel. "I need to talk to Robert," she said to Mrs. Bamford.

Mrs. Bamford sighed and handed the phone to Robert.

"Any changes?" Mabel asked. "Did you stay up all night?"

"I . . . uh . . . well, not exactly," admitted Robert.

Sam came into the room wearing a towel. "Who are you talking to?" he asked.

"Mabel," said Robert.

"Is that Sam?" asked Mabel. "Look at his teeth. Are they longer?"

"I can't tell," said Robert. "And I'm not supposed to be talking about teeth. I've got to go."

Sam started to get dressed. Robert was still studying his brother for signs of vampiredom.

Mrs. Bamford had fresh bagels for them in the living room. "Garlic-onion for you?" she asked Sam.

Sam shook his head. "No, I don't feel like garlic this morning," he said. "I think I'll have plain."

"Uh-oh," said Robert.

"Uh-oh what?" asked Sam.

"Nothing," said Robert. But he filed it away. He would have to tell Mabel that his brother suddenly didn't like garlic—just the way Vlad's whole family didn't. Mabel had told him that all vampires hated the smell of garlic—and now, the morning after being bitten by Vlad, Sam didn't want a garlic bagel. Robert shook his head. It wasn't going to be easy living with a brother who was a vampire.

PLEASE, PLEASE HELP ME

On the way to the tournament, Robert told Mabel that Sam had not wanted his usual garlic bagel that morning.

"That's the sign we were looking for," warned Mabel. "We'll have to watch him like hawks."

At the tournament, Sam barely paid any attention to Mabel and Robert. His whole being was focused on Vlad. Instead of row upon row of chessboards, there were just two chessboards and four chairs on the podium. Buddy Ryan easily beat his first opponent. But Vlad's semi-final match was a struggle. He was playing a middle-aged woman who made a clicking noise with her teeth every time she made a move. The noise seemed to bother Vlad, but in the end he won.

Sam stood up and cheered. The judges came out and removed two chairs and one chessboard. Now it would be just Vlad against Buddy Ryan, one of the best chess players in the world. A huge screen was set up behind the chessboard so the moves could be shown. The championship was to be broadcast on cable TV and the great hall was now brightly lit. Vlad blinked as if the bright lights bothered him more than his last opponent's clicking teeth.

Buddy Ryan was sitting back in his chair, chewing gum, looking very relaxed. Vlad sat opposite him, looking very pale. Vlad's feet barely touched the ground, and he swung his feet back and forth.

Sam looked down at the podium. Vlad looked so nervous. Sam wished he could be there with his friend.

The game started. Vlad had drawn white, so he moved a pawn. Buddy Ryan pushed one of his pawns up to block Vlad. Vlad moved another pawn. In the very next move, Buddy moved his knight, in a surprise attack. Vlad's head snapped back as if he had been slapped, even though Buddy hadn't touched him. Now Vlad's king was open to attack.

"They might as well light the Empire State Building red, white, and blue," said a man sitting next to Sam.

"Not so fast," said Sam. Slowly, Vlad fought back. For a while it looked as if the game might be a draw. The players moved their pieces around the board—neither giving up much. The game went on for five hours.

Sam and the rest of the audience were exhausted from watching. Suddenly, Vlad made a move with one of his own knights. Now it was Buddy Ryan's turn to look stunned. Sweat broke out on the American's forehead. He stared at the chess set, but there was no escape.

The television announcer was whispering into his microphone, "The young boy from Romania just made a brilliant, creative move. Absolute genius!"

Slowly, Buddy moved his right hand and toppled his own king, admitting that Vlad had won. Then he reached across the chessboard to shake Vlad's hand. The audience burst into applause.

Vlad's shoulders slumped. He didn't look triumphant. He looked as if he were the one who had lost. His eyes searched the balcony as if desperate for help. Sam tried to wave at him.

Mrs. Bamford hugged Sam. "That was spectacular," she said. "Come on. Vlad's parents got us tickets to a special VIP reception."

As they made their way down from the balcony, they heard the announcer say, "Ladies and gentlemen, boys and girls. All of you holding red tickets are invited to the special winners' ceremony to be held across the street at the Empire State Building. We will all celebrate our young Romanian champion, Vlad Clinciu."

Sam and his family found their way through the crowd to where Vlad was standing cornered by TV reporters. Vlad looked up at Sam with the same desperate look in his eyes that Sam had noticed before.

"No more questions, ladies and gentlemen," said the organizer of the tournament. "You may continue across the street at the

Empire State Building."

Vlad reached a hand out for Sam. "Stay close to me, please," he begged.

"What's wrong?" asked Sam. "This should be the happiest day of your life."

Vlad didn't answer. The crowd was pushing them along to the Empire State Building. The match had continued nearly all afternoon. Now, in early November, New York was dark by five o'clock.

Once inside, a special elevator had been set aside for the winners of the chess tournament and the VIPs. As Vlad, Sam, and their families zipped up in the elevator, Vlad looked more and more scared.

"They . . . they . . ." stammered Vlad. "I should never have won. Please help me. . . ."

"Vlad, what are you talking about?" asked Sam. "It's time to tell me your secret. You must tell me."

"You are right," said Vlad. "I will tell only you."

As the elevator doors opened, Vlad started to whisper into Sam's ear.

"*No!*" screamed Robert. He lunged at Vlad.

He couldn't let his brother be bitten by a vampire again.

"What are you doing?" Sam exclaimed.

"He's a vampire!" shouted Mabel. "And he's turning you into one. That's why he bit you! He was going to bite you again."

Vlad looked at Sam sadly. Then he ran out of the elevator and disappeared around a corner.

"See," said Mabel triumphantly. "There's proof. Only a vampire would run away."

"He's not a vampire," said Sam determinedly. "He had a secret that he needed to tell me . . . and now you've scared him away. I've got to find him."

"Vampires stick together," Mabel said to Robert.

Robert didn't know what to believe. He hated to think that his brother was now more loyal to a vampire than to him. But it looked as if Mabel might be right again.

10

ANYTHING'S POSSIBLE

On the observation deck, before Sam had a chance to slip away and look for Vlad, one of the reporters asked Mabel if she knew Vlad personally.

"Yes, I do," said Mabel.

Sam clapped his hand over her mouth. "If you say one thing about Vlad being a vampire, I swear I will turn you into a vampire right here and now," he whispered into her ear.

Mabel swallowed.

"Do you understand?" warned Sam.

Mabel nodded.

Sam removed his hand. "My cousin had a little food on her lips. I didn't want to her to be embarrassed," he said quickly.

Mabel gave Sam a dirty look. She turned to the reporter. "I myself am a very good chess player. . . . Well, maybe not as good as Vlad . . . but someday. Nadia, Vlad's sister, and I are e-mail buddies."

Nadia came up to them. "Where's Vlad?" she asked. "Everybody's looking for him."

"I don't know," said Sam. "He was looking scared, and he wanted to tell me something, but then he ran away."

"We have to find him," said Nadia.

"Ladies and gentlemen," said the announcer. "Would our winner, Vlad Clinciu, make his way to the podium?"

There was silence as everybody looked around for Vlad.

Then Sam noticed that the door to the men's restroom was swinging, as if someone had just opened it. "He must be in there," Sam said to Robert, Mabel, and Nadia. "Wait here."

Robert, of course, followed Sam into the men's room, but the stalls looked empty. Then Sam looked under the doors. In the last stall, he saw a pair of feet drawn up on the toilet.

"Vlad?" asked Sam.

"Go away," begged Vlad.

"Everybody's looking for you," said Sam.

"I know. I can't answer questions," said Vlad.

"You told me you wanted help. And you said it was time to tell me your secret. Well, you don't have any time left," warned Sam.

"Mabel and I already know your secret," said Robert. "You're a vampire. You wanted Sam to be a vampire, too. That's why you bit him. And it's working. Sam didn't want a garlic bagel this morning."

"What?" exclaimed Vlad. "I don't want anybody to be a vampire. I'm scared of vampires. And I didn't bite Sam."

"How can he be scared of them if he is one?" Robert asked Sam.

"He's not a vampire," said Sam. "Are you, Vlad?"

"I'm not a vampire!" said Vlad.

"You're not?" asked Robert. "But your

teeth are pointy. You don't like to play chess during the day. And you don't like garlic."

Vlad opened the door to the toilet stall. He shook his head and put his hands up to his forehead. "It's hopeless," he said. "It's even worse than I expected. Sam, if even your brother and cousin think I'm a vampire, what will the rest of the world think? I should never have won the match."

Vlad started to cry. Sam looked at Robert. "You made him cry."

"Do real vampires cry?" Robert asked.

"You're an idiot," said Sam. "Can't you tell he's not a vampire? Vlad, come on, buddy. Everybody in America isn't like Mabel. She convinced my brother with her vampire stories, but most people don't pay any attention to her. She's just a little girl who dresses funny, like your sister."

"Nadia and I resent that remark," said Mabel, marching into the men's room, holding Nadia's hand.

"You two can't be in here," shrieked Robert. "It's a men's room!"

"So, go guard the door," ordered Mabel.

"Nadia just told me the truth. Vlad and Nadia's mother's maiden name was Tepes. They really are descended from the original Vlad the Impaler . . . the original Count Dracul. Vlad is afraid everyone will think he's a vampire."

"But everybody does," wailed Vlad. "You do . . . and Robert does. Soon the whole world will think I'm a vampire."

"Well," said Robert slowly, "it was Mabel who got me thinking that way. And Mabel is often wrong."

"I resent that remark," said Mabel.

"You resemble that remark," muttered Sam.

"All my schoolmates warned me that if Americans found out about my family background I would be in deep trouble." Vlad sniffed. "Sam, that's the secret I didn't want to tell you. I'm a very, very distant great-great-nephew," said Vlad, "of the real Count Dracul. And when I said I had big nerves, I do. I just threw up."

"Mabel," said Robert, "I don't think real vampires cry when their feelings are hurt."

Mabel sighed. "You might be right," she admitted. "Maybe we got a little carried away. I don't think real vampires cry and throw up."

"On my honor," wailed Vlad. "I am not a vampire. In my country, we do not believe that the original Count Vlad was a vampire. He was a cruel man, but he was fighting for our freedom against a cruel enemy. However, I cannot deny that he was my relative."

"Well, in America, nobody has to take the blame for their relatives," said Sam. He looked pointedly at Mabel.

Mabel gave them all a huffy look. "Come on, Nadia," she said. "I don't think you and I should be in the men's room with these smelly boys."

Vlad sighed. "I guess I have to face the music. I'm sorry, Sam. I'm afraid I embarrassed you . . . my American friend."

"I keep telling you, Vlad. We all have relatives who embarrass us."

Robert looked up at his older brother. "Do you mean me?"

"Well, sometimes," said Sam. Then he saw how anxious Robert was. "Not all the time," he whispered.

They went outside. Vlad took the podium. "I want to thank everybody in America for being so kind to me," he said. "I have an American friend, Sam Bamford. Sam is a beginner, and he played chess with me on-line. And he made me a better player because he just loved chess, the way I loved chess at the beginning before I had to take it so seriously. Sam told me jokes . . . and I had fun. I think I won because of Sam. I know he wanted me to win even though he is an American—and he is my friend."

"Is he here?" asked one reporter. "Let's get a picture of the two of you together."

"I don't know," said Vlad.

Sam made his way through the crowd. "I'm here," he said. He went up on the podium. He gave Vlad a hug. Sam wasn't afraid to hug him now; he wasn't even afraid of Vlad's teeth.

Then Mabel and Nadia jumped on the stage. "Actually," Mabel said, "as I told you all before, I am a friend of Vlad's sister, Nadia. Girls can play chess, too. And as you can see, by dressing in black and white, I have the perfect outfit. I think outfits are important. I buy many of them at thrift shops. You don't have to spend a lot of money, but it's important to dress for the occasion."

Sam rolled his eyes. "I told you nobody's responsible for their relatives," Sam told Vlad.

Vlad nodded to him. "Thank you, my friend," he whispered.

The director of Public Relations for the Empire State Building explained to Vlad, and everyone present, that electricians had already put color gels the size of giant pizzas on the spotlights.

"In your honor, the top of the Empire State Building will now be the colors of the Romanian flag," she said. And suddenly the building was bathed in blue, yellow, and red lights. Vlad thanked her.

"It is a proud moment for my country," said Mr. Clinciu.

"I'm proud of you, too," Sam said to Vlad.

Just then a pigeon flew by in the night. Its wings were outspread.

"Was that a pigeon or a bat?" Robert whispered to Sam.

"A pigeon," said Sam, but the truth was that he wasn't quite sure.

Vlad took out his camera and tried to photograph the pigeon. The bird's wing caught the light and threw a huge shadow over them all.

"That's some New York pigeon," said Vlad.

"I'm not sure what it was," whispered Sam. "New York pigeons usually sleep during the night."

"Maybe it's a Romanian pigeon," said Vlad. "Maybe it's proud because I won today."

"Anything's possible," said Robert.

DATE			
9 5	15 20	20 20	10 10

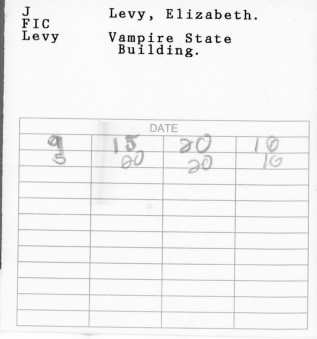

J
FIC
Levy

Levy, Elizabeth.

Vampire State
Building.

DATE			
9 5	15 20	20 20	10 10